CHRISTMAS IN JULY

- SCREENPLAY -

JAY ASHER

faulty bracket PUBLISHING

First edition: October 2019

ISBN 978-1-7340397-1-9 (paperback)
ISBN 978-1-7340397-0-2 (ebook)

ALSO BY JAY ASHER

NOVELS

Thirteen Reasons Why

The Future of Us
(co-author: Carolyn Mackler)

What Light

GRAPHIC NOVEL

Piper
(co-author: Jessica Freeburg;
illustrator: Jeff Stokely)

TO:

ISAIAH ASHER
&
JOYCE C. HALL

TABLE OF CONTENTS

AUTHOR'S NOTE

After I published my first novel, a very serious high school drama (*Thirteen Reasons Why*), people asked if there was another genre I wanted to write someday. I always answered, "Yes, a Christmas romance." They thought I was joking. When I later published a teen romance set on a Christmas tree lot (*What Light*), they finally realized I had been sincere.

Writing that book, I did two things to keep me wrapped in the Christmas spirit no matter the season, and because we don't have true seasons where I live in California. First, I lit scented candles (evergreen tree or gingerbread cookie). Second, I played non-stop country Christmas tunes (Alan Jackson's *Let it be Christmas* and Lady Antebellum's *On This Winter's Night* albums were great companions).

As someone who seeks Christmas love stories regardless of the medium, I eagerly await the flurry of them on television each winter. While writing *What Light* to some great holiday songs, immersed in a story of love taking root, the idea for a Christmas movie-within-a-movie starring a country music singer took hold. I took a break from writing my book and wrote the following script.

Author's Note

After finishing the story and choosing to publish it as a book, I considered novelizing the screenplay first. But to keep the concept of the movie-within-a-movie clear and fun, I decided...no!

Whatever season you read it in, I hope the story of Amanda and Cole makes it feel like the coziest Christmas in your heart.

- Jay

READING A SCREENPLAY

Sample Scene

INT. AMANDA'S HOUSE / OFFICE - NIGHT

Cole looks at the framed DVDs of Amanda's Christmas movies.

COLE
I bet I've seen all of these. Some of them
twice.

How to Read that Scene

INT.(inside) or EXT.(outside) SETTING - DAY or NIGHT
[indicates the start of a new scene]

This is what a character does and what the camera sees.

CHARACTER NAME
This is what the character says.

ACT I

Fade in:

INT. AMANDA'S HOUSE / OFFICE - DAY

Like a musician's framed gold record, a framed DVD case and disc from a TV Christmas romance hangs on a wall. Within that frame is also a sprig of mistletoe. The wintery DVD artwork shows AMANDA, late 30s, hugging a male actor. Next to that frame is a frame for another TV Christmas romance with similar imagery (but Amanda with a different male actor) and another mistletoe. And then another frame of another Christmas romance and Amanda with another man. This set-up repeats with another frame, and another, and...

Next to the last frame, a second-story window overlooks a swimming pool. Amanda, in a sundress and sunglasses, sits with her legs in the pool. From beside her, PATRICK, 10 years old, leaps into the pool. Cannonball!

EXT. AMANDA'S HOUSE / POOL – DAY

Amanda is splashed by Patrick's cannonball. She laughs and, when he comes up, splashes him with her foot.

PATRICK
Wait! I don't want to get wet!

She splashes him again.

AMANDA
And that's for being sarcastic to your
mom.

Sitting at an umbrella-shaded table, OWEN, mid-40s, flips the page in a script. More scripts are scattered on the glass tabletop.

OWEN
Most of these will be cast within a few
weeks, so we need to choose now.
You know, before Christmas.

AMANDA
Do any require me to audition?

Patrick is about to splash her with his arm.

AMANDA
Don't you dare.

OWEN
The ones we're interested in would love
to have you. All you need to do is say
yes.

Amanda raises her eyebrow at Patrick: See? Momma's still got it.

He splashes her.

AMANDA
What can I say? When you got it, you
got it. Easy Street!

PATRICK
Mom, they're Christmas romances. I
think you mean Cheesy Street.

AMANDA
Sentimental does not mean cheesy…
necessarily.

Owen holds up his thumb and index finger to Patrick: They can be a little cheesy.

OWEN
We can probably put it in her contract
that you get a cameo.

PATRICK
Really?!

AMANDA
Oh, now you're interested.

She gives Owen a dirty look.

AMANDA
Put on the hat while we do this. It's
good luck!

Owen sighs and picks up a Santa hat from the chair beside him. He puts it on and then flicks the fuzzy white ball which has a bell inside.

AMANDA
(to Patrick)
And, no. If you want to act, you can join
a school play first.
Besides, I promised your dad he could
watch you while I'm on set.

OWEN
Do you want the loglines for my top
five?

Amanda leans back, enjoying the warmth of the sun.

OWEN
(reading)
"Two divorcees on a Caribbean
Christmas cruise..."

Patrick rolls his eyes and lets himself sink below the water.

INT. CONCERT / BACKSTAGE – DAY

Fans cheer wildly. COLE, late 30s, descends the stairs from a brightly lit stage. Clean shaven, he wears tight jeans, tucked black t-shirt, cowboy boots, and no hat. He hands his guitar to a ROADIE. The rest of the band comes down the stairs after him, congratulating each other.

KRISTIN, late-20s, approaches.

KRISTIN
Sounding great today, Cole.

COLE
Man, listen to them! That sure helps.

The cheers turn to chants.

AUDIENCE *(off-screen)*
Cole! Cole! Cole!

The Roadie hands Cole a new guitar and helps him strap it on. MISS HEARTBREAKER, early 40s, runs up and holds a voice recorder close to Cole's mouth.

COLE
Ah, Miss Heartbreaker. It's been awhile.

MISS HEARTBREAKER
Rumor has it you're going after Amanda
Fox to co-star in a secret movie project.
Care to comment?

KRISTIN
I'm sorry, Cole's not going to—

COLE
Sure. Where did you hear that?

Kristin smiles and takes a step back.

MISS HEARTBREAKER
Anonymous tip. So, I went through
some of your early interviews. You had
a major crush on her in high school.

COLE
On the character she played. Yes, I did.

MISS HEARTBREAKER
Is this an attempt to—?

COLE
No, I am not trying to fulfill a teenage
crush on a celebrity.

MISS HEARTBREAKER
Because my readers would love—

COLE
Oh, I know your slogan. "Make outs,
make ups, and break ups. If it makes a
famous heart beat..."

MISS HEARTBREAKER
"I break it first." Now, if this movie does
happen—

COLE
Then you know how to find me. You've
more than proven that.

*Miss Heartbreaker clicks off her recorder. The Roadie starts pushing
Cole toward the stairs.*

COLE
(to Kristin)
Did you hear from Amanda's people?

Kristin shakes her head.

COLE
I thought she loved doing these movies.

KRISTIN
She does one a year. And she probably
has a million to choose from.

COLE
It's a great script!

KRISTIN
I'll call again.

Cole follows his Band back to the stage. The chants turn to cheers again.

EXT. AMANDA'S HOUSE / POOL - DAY

Amanda and Owen snack on a fruit plate at the table.

OWEN
We're down to three scripts. We can do
this.

His phone rings. He looks at it, grunts, and silences it.

AMANDA
Who was that?

OWEN
Okay, there is one script I didn't tell you
about. And they've been very persistent.

AMANDA
Why didn't you tell me about it?

OWEN
Because you have certain...prejudices.

AMANDA
(laughing)
What?!

OWEN
It's about a country music star—

AMANDA
What do I have against country music?
I may not listen to it...

OWEN
And it stars a country music star.

She considers this.

AMANDA
Oh.

Owen nods.

Amanda pushes back her chair, stands, and paces.

AMANDA
That makes me so mad! Musicians think
just because they made a few music
videos—where they play themselves, by
the way—they can suddenly be the lead
in a feature film...television movie...
whatever. It's so...so...

OWEN
So, you're saying I should have told you
about this one?

Amanda returns to her seat.

OWEN
It is a good script.

AMANDA
Like you said, we're down to three.

INT. CONCERT / BACKSTAGE - DAY

The Band descends the stairs as the crowd cheers. Cole comes down last this time and hands his guitar to the Roadie.

COLE
Now that's how we do it!
Awesome job, everyone.

Kristin gives Cole a towel and walks beside him as they follow the Band down a hall. Cole wipes at his forehead and chest.

COLE
Anything?

KRISTIN
I texted back and forth with her agent. I told him we have actresses lining up for this part but we're holding out for her.

COLE
I had it written for her!

KRISTIN
I told him that.

COLE
Do you think it's because I'm a singer?
Maybe she thinks I'm not serious.

KRISTIN

I don't know what to tell you, Cole.

He considers his options.

COLE
You can find out her address and tell me
that.

Kristin doesn't understand.

COLE
I don't have a show tomorrow. I'll fly
out and see what her holdup is.

INT. AMANDA'S HOUSE / LIVING ROOM – NIGHT

On the TV is a movie starring BELINDA, late 30s. Onscreen, she walks down a busy sidewalk talking on her phone.

BELINDA
(acting)
I don't know, but he hasn't dated
anyone seriously in ten years. Ten years!
He spends all his free time volunteering
at the animal shelter.

INT. AMANDA'S HOUSE / KITCHEN – NIGHT

Amanda, behind the kitchen island, pours wine for JESSICA and NATALIE, late 30s, sitting on stools. They each have a copy of the same book in front of them. Belinda's movie plays in the adjoining room.

JESSICA
Well, I did not like the book, but it did
make a road trip sound nice.

Amanda holds up her glass, a cheers to that idea. Jessica and Natalie raise their glasses.

NATALIE
We so deserve that.

AMANDA
Yes, we do.

They each sip their wine. The doorbell rings.

Amanda leaves to answer the front door, which can be seen from the kitchen. She calls over her shoulder...

AMANDA
And I'm calling shotgun right now.

INT. AMANDA'S HOUSE / FOYER - NIGHT

Amanda opens the door. Cole wears a button-down shirt, sleeves cuffed just below the elbows. At the sight of Amanda, he smiles.

COLE
I got the right address!

AMANDA
I'm sorry, I'm in the middle of a book
club right now. Plus, I don't sign
autographs for people who just show up
at—

COLE
Autograph? No…
(understanding)
I see.
I know who you are, but—

Jessica and Natalie run up to the door.

JESSICA
You're Cole Buskin!

NATALIE
Do you want to join our book club?!

JESSICA
You don't even have to read!

AMANDA
Forgive them. They're drunk.
Wait… You're Cole Buskin?

JESSICA
That's what I said!

AMANDA
The musician? With the Christmas
movie?

COLE
That's right, *A Christmas Single*.
I flew halfway across the country to see if
you'll do it.

Amanda is confused, but Natalie and Jessica are in awe.

NATALIE
That's commitment.

Jessica opens the door wider.

JESSICA
Come in!

Cole follows Jessica and Natalie into the house.

AMANDA
(*to self*)
Odd. I thought this was my house.

INT. AMANDA'S HOUSE / KITCHEN - NIGHT

Cole drinks a glass of water while the women drink wine.

COLE
When I was in high school—and I
would not admit this to the guys—but I
was a huge fan of *Homeroom.*

AMANDA
Thank you.

COLE
I was in the same graduating class you
were supposed to be in.
Of course, I knew you were all older
than your characters.

AMANDA
Not that much older.

COLE
And, because I was a fan—because I am
a fan—I had the part written for you.

NATALIE
For her?

COLE
Other actresses could do it, but I asked
the writer to picture you when he wrote
it.

JESSICA
Oh, right! Because you totally crushed
on her in high school.
I read that in an interview.
(off Amanda)
I didn't tell you because you don't like
country music.

AMANDA
Country music is...fine, but I'm not too
keen on the public knowing you "totally
crushed on me" at one point.

Cole laughs

COLE
I would think that'd help the ratings.

AMANDA
I'm sure it would.
Look, my son played t-ball with a kid
whose dad was on *Homeroom* with
me. And wouldn't you know it, right

after my divorce, little Miss
Heartbreaker—

Cole crosses his arms.

AMANDA
She shows up at a game hoping our TV
romance would now bloom in the real
world.
He and I are friends but I didn't sit with
him because I didn't want our photo
bringing more celebrity gossips to my
son's next game.

COLE
I respect that.

JESSICA
I see your face plastered everywhere
with lots of famous women.
Let's see, there's Coleissa, Colennifer,
Elizacole…

NATALIE
Weren't you already in a Colemanda?

COLE
Most of them were just friends.

Amanda nods: Exactly.

AMANDA
And what do you mean you had this
written?

COLE
Well, I'm a country music star, not an
actor.

*Amanda lifts her glass, a cheers to that statement, and then downs
the rest of her wine.*

COLE
With some hit songs, I knew I could
make this happen. And stars fade fast,
so I didn't wait.

JESSICA
Okay, let me throw this out there. It's a
thing I've heard some actors complain
about musicians.

Natalie shakes her head.

NATALIE
Jessica…

JESSICA
You're in the music biz. That's good. But
what makes you think you can act?

*Cole smirks at Amanda. She grabs the bottle of wine and refills her
glass.*

COLE
The movie is about a country singer
who's seeking inspiration for a song.
I know that guy pretty well.

AMANDA

A role so close to home can make it hard
to act honestly or with vulnerability.

COLE
Two things that have never been
difficult for me: honesty and
vulnerability.

NATALIE
You are so hot.

Jessica touches Natalie's arm.

JESSICA
Honey, you said that out loud.

AMANDA
So, I'll need to act like I can fall in love
with a man in a cowboy hat?

COLE
We don't all wear cowboy hats, you
know. And before you ask, I haven't
worn rhinestones in years.
But, since you brought up honesty, did
you even consider my script?

Amanda ponders telling him the truth.

AMANDA
Let me show you something.

INT. AMANDA'S HOUSE / OFFICE - NIGHT

Cole looks at the framed DVDs of Amanda's Christmas movies.

COLE
I bet I've seen all of these. Some of them
twice.

Amanda sits on a couch.

AMANDA
You have not.

COLE
Why is that hard to believe?
Haven't you heard? Every cowboy has a
soft side.

AMANDA
Okay then, which one is your favorite?

*He steps back to look them over. After deep consideration, he points
to* O, Little Star of Bethany.

COLE
I'm sure it was the situation going on in
my own life, but when I saw that…
(chokes up)
When Bethany's neighbor—

AMANDA
The girl in the hospital?

Cole puts his hands on his hips and lets out a deep breath.

COLE
She reminded me of my niece.

She was so brave, just like Bethany.

Amanda leans forward, concerned.

COLE
I'll be honest, it was hard to finish that one.

AMANDA
You don't have to talk about it. I understand.

Cole turns to her and breaks into a grin.

COLE
Then you'll understand that was some mighty fine acting for a music man, don't you think?

AMANDA
Oh, no you did not! You preyed on my emotions.
And you used your niece!

COLE
What? I don't even have a niece.
I just imagined what it'd feel like if that happened to my dog. That's what actors do, right?

Cole sits beside her.

AMANDA
Yes, that was some mighty fine acting.

COLE
Thank you.

AMANDA
So, Cole, why a Christmas romance?

COLE
For starters, I love Christmas.
But more than that, some of my fondest
memories with my mom—

AMANDA
You are not allowed to prey on my
emotions again.

COLE
I do have a mom and she is still alive.
I promise.

Amanda nods: Please continue.

COLE
One of my favorite Christmas traditions
is watching these movies with her.
She just loves them! As do I, but I really
love watching them with her.
Now, to see her son star in one? That'd
be the best Christmas present ever.

She studies him: He's being serious.

AMANDA
No.

Cole looks puzzled.

AMANDA
I did not consider your script. I haven't
even read it.

Cole smiles weakly and stands up. He walks to the frames.

COLE
Tell me about the mistletoe in these
frames.

Amanda joins him.

AMANDA
Every Christmas romance needs a first
kiss, right? Well, mine were beneath
these.

COLE
These are the actual mistletoe you kissed
under?

AMANDA
Sometimes they were used in the scene,
but if the story didn't call for mistletoe I
had one hung out of view on the boom
mic.
I'm sorry, a boom mic is—

COLE
I know what a boom mic is.
So, these were your good luck charms?

AMANDA
One of my special Christmas traditions.

She continues looking at the frames while he looks at her.

COLE
Will you at least look at my script?

She looks at him. Into his eyes.

INT. AMANDA'S HOUSE / KITCHEN - NIGHT

On the stove, a teapot whistles. Amanda turns off the burner and pours the hot water into a mug.

Searching through a cupboard, pushing aside boxes of tea, she finds one marked "Christmas Time Tea." She tears open a packet and lowers the bag into her mug.

Amanda dims the lights above the kitchen island. She sets her mug of tea beside an unread script: A Christmas Single. *Near the script are two scented candles: gingerbread and evergreen.*

She lights both candles and then wafts the scent toward her face. She sits on a stool and flips to the first page.

LATER

Halfway through the script, Amanda flips another page.

Patrick carries the steaming teapot and refills his mom's mug as she continues to read.

LATER

The mug is empty. Amanda finishes the last page in the script. She flips the entire script over so the title shows: A Christmas Single. *She stares at it and exhales.*

PATRICK *(off-screen)*
Is that the one?

Amanda looks at Patrick. Wearing pajamas, he stands at the kitchen entrance.

She smiles and holds out an arm, calling him to her. Patrick walks over and gives her a kiss.

PATRICK
I'm glad you found one you like.

She watches him go and then looks back at the script.

AMANDA
(to self)
I love it.

INT. AMANDA'S HOUSE / BEDROOM - DAY

Amanda pulls two dresses from her closet. Looking them over, she can't decide between them so lays both in an already-full suitcase on her bed.

Owen sits on the edge of the bed reviewing a printed itinerary.

OWEN
They'll have a driver waiting when you land. I included his number in case you don't find each other.

Amanda returns to her closet.

AMANDA
A driver? Wow. They're splurging compared to the last few movies. Too bad they aren't splurging for an on-set acting coach.

OWEN
I don't think you have to worry about
Cole. They wouldn't have splurged a
dime if they didn't believe in him.
More importantly, he needs to know
you believe in him.

AMANDA
I'm an actress. I get paid to make people
believe me.

OWEN
Plus, they plan to do a lot of Method
Acting with him.

She turns to Owen.

AMANDA
They're bringing in real snow?

OWEN
Don't be silly.
For example, he's supposed to be taken
aback when he first sees you. So, they're
going to keep you two apart until the
moment you open the door and—

AMANDA
But we've already met.

OWEN
It's the small things. That added look of
surprise. Like a groom not seeing his
bride on their wedding day until the
ceremony.

AMANDA
As long as I don't open the door to a
rhinestone cowboy.
No, I'm sure we'll be fine. I don't have a
bit of concern.

OWEN
Good.

AMANDA
I'm kidding. That was just some mighty
fine acting on my part.

INT. DRESSING ROOM - NIGHT

*In the make-up trailer, the counter is strung with Christmas lights.
Three mirrors are framed with shiny red garland and the edges of
the glass appear covered in frost. Cole is seated on the middle stool
(the other two are empty) with a salon cape over his clothes. The
MAKE-UP ARTIST dabs a cloth against his five o'clock shadow.*

Kristin enters and stands beside Cole. She talks to his reflection.

KRISTIN
You've got about five minutes.

COLE
How's everyone doing?

KRISTIN
They finished the telephone scene inside
the bed-and-breakfast. Now they're
setting the lights for your grand reveal.

COLE
How's Amanda? Is she nervous?

KRISTIN
Should she be?

COLE
It's no secret she's apprehensive about
acting with a musician.

KRISTIN
She'll be fine. And you'll be fine.

COLE
I'm only praying I don't mess up my
first scene. If we can get through that
and she's happy, I think my own jitters
will die down.

A warning knock at the door. The Make-Up Artist removes Cole's cape.

MAKE-UP ARTIST
There you are.

Cole stands and nervously shakes out his hands.

The Make-Up Artist hands him a cowboy hat. Looking in the mirror, Cole puts it on.

KRISTIN
Transformation complete.

Cole smirks.

COLE

She is going to hate this.

EXT. BED & BREAKFAST / PORCH - NIGHT

On the porch, Cole faces a closed front door, an acoustic guitar case at his feet.

Also on the porch, a CAMERA OPERATOR steadies a bulky camera on his shoulder. Against the railing, the SCRIPT SUPERVISOR jots notes into her binder.

In the front yard, several CREW MEMBERS spray the lawn with fake snow. The DIRECTOR, mid-50s, climbs the porch steps.

> **DIRECTOR**
> Everyone here is real excited to see our
> lovebirds meet.
> How are you feeling?

Cole looks back at the lawn.

> **COLE**
> Well, it's beginning to feel a lot like
> Christmas.

> **DIRECTOR**
> That's our job.
> Okay, Amanda's all set. All you have to
> do is knock, wait a few seconds for her
> to get to the door, and...

EXT. NEXT DOOR TO BED & BREAKFAST / PORCH - NIGHT

A burly BODYGUARD marches up the walkway to the porch. Miss Heartbreaker, partially concealed behind a post, aims her camera toward the film-shoot next door.

BODYGUARD
Miss Heartbreaker, hello.

Defeated, she puts down her camera.

MISS HEARTBREAKER
I was so close.

The Bodyguard steps onto the porch.

BODYGUARD
This is part of our closed set. You can't
be here.

MISS HEARTBREAKER
Um... I'm with the press?

BODYGUARD
That's a stretch.

EXT. BED & BREAKFAST / PORCH - NIGHT

The Director adjusts the rim of Cole's hat.

DIRECTOR
To really dramatize this moment, let's
have you looking down when she opens
the door.
Knock, then look down. Got it?

COLE
I'll look down like I'm wiping my boots
on the mat.

DIRECTOR
That's fine. And when the door opens,
pause...lift your head...and smile!
Amanda will say her line, you say yours,
and we cut.

Cole nods and the Director walks behind the Camera Operator.

DIRECTOR
Snow please!

Crew Members on the roof above the porch scatter snow in the air. Cole picks up the guitar case.

DIRECTOR
Action!

EXT. NEXT DOOR TO BED & BREAKFAST / PORCH - NIGHT

The Bodyguard holds down Miss Heartbreaker's camera. He puts a finger to his lips.

They both watch the scene being filmed at the house next door.

EXT. BED & BREAKFAST / PORCH - NIGHT

Filming: *Cole closes his eyes and exhales.*

Ready, he knocks on the door.

He looks down, scuffing the bottoms of his boots on the doormat.

INT. BED & BREAKFAST / FOYER – NIGHT

Filming: *Amanda walks to the door and opens it.*

The lowered cowboy hat conceals Cole's face. The cowboy hat slowly lifts and his gorgeous gaze overwhelms Amanda.

Awkward silence.

EXT. BED & BREAKFAST / PORCH - NIGHT

Filming:

The Director is puzzled: Why isn't Amanda saying her line?

COLE
(to Amanda)
I'm sorry, I must have the wrong house.
Are they filming a movie around here?

DIRECTOR
Cut!

The Script Supervisor stifles a laugh. Amanda steps onto the porch and looks at the Director.

AMANDA
It was the hat!

Cole feigns confusion.

AMANDA
(to Cole)
You don't wear a cowboy hat!

COLE
I'm an actor. I'm acting like I wear a
cowboy hat.

AMANDA
No, that is not fair.

The Director whispers to the Camera Operator.

DIRECTOR
At least we have chemistry.

EXT. NEXT DOOR TO BED & BREAKFAST / PORCH - NIGHT

The Bodyguard watches the scene with a smirk.

MISS HEARTBREAKER
So very close.

COMMERCIAL BREAK

ACT II

INT. BED & BREAKFAST / DINING ROOM - DAY

Filming: *Cole sits at a dining room table. Amanda sets a plate of scrambled eggs, bacon, toast, and fruit in front of him.*

COLE
(acting)
Looks delicious. Thank you.

AMANDA
(acting)
It would be hard to find musical
inspiration on an empty stomach.

She slides the salt and pepper closer to him. At the opposite end of the table, an ELDERLY MAN and WOMAN eat the same breakfast.

ELDERLY MAN
(acting)
I've never been much for country music
myself.

ELDERLY WOMAN
(acting)
Darling!

ELDERLY MAN
(acting)
Oh, that's not rude! You can't be into
everything.

The Elderly Man stuffs a forkful of eggs into his mouth.

COLE
(acting)
It's true. You like what you like. Some
country music doesn't speak to me, but
there's a lot of variation in any genre.

ELDERLY MAN
(acting)
It all sounds the same to me.

AMANDA
(acting)
I think I'll go wash some dishes.

Amanda leaves through a door to the kitchen.

DIRECTOR *(off-screen)*
And...cut!

The Elderly Man lifts a napkin and spits his egg into it.

ELDERLY MAN
Can we pop my plate in the microwave
if I have to eat any more of this?

He holds the plate out to his side. An ASSISTANT rushes in to take the plate and carries it into the kitchen.

Amanda walks out of the kitchen. Cole is getting his make-up retouched by the Make-Up Artist.

COLE
I'm not doing too bad, am I?

Amanda smiles.

AMANDA
Not at all.

The Elderly Woman eats a grape from her plate. The Script Supervisor quickly replaces it with another grape.

SCRIPT SUPERVISOR
Let's eat those only when we're rolling.

ELDERLY WOMAN
I am so sorry! I keep forgetting.

SCRIPT SUPERVISOR
If you're hungry, I'll get you something
that's not part of the scene.
(to Amanda)
They need you in wardrobe. The next
scene is dessert with Cole.

AMANDA
(to Cole)
This is the one I warned you about.

COLE
(to Make-Up Artist)

Do they really use mashed potato for ice
cream?

MAKE-UP ARTIST
So it doesn't melt under the lights.
But the cherries are real!

COLE
That's how I like my potatoes. With
fruit.

*Amanda leaves. The Elderly Woman eats another grape. The Script
Supervisor replaces the grape.*

ELDERLY WOMAN
Sorry.

EXT. BED & BREAKFAST - DAY

*A SET DESIGNER hangs thick black fabric outside the window to
the dining room.*

INT. BED & BREAKFAST / DINING ROOM - NIGHT

*The black fabric outside the window is adjusted until it looks like
night.*

*Alone at the table, Cole turns a page in his script. A PROP
PERSON lights a candle in the center of the table.*

DIRECTOR
Everyone ready?

Cole hands his script to the Assistant.

LATER

Filming: *Pull back from the candle flame. Cole sits at the table. He hangs his hat on the empty chair beside him.*

Amanda enters from the kitchen carrying two sundae glasses with ice cream and cherries.

> **AMANDA**
> *(acting)*
> Mind if I join you?

> **COLE**
> *(acting)*
> Please.

Amanda sets one sundae in front of Cole. She sets the other in front of the adjacent chair and sits down.

Cole eats a spoonful of ice cream.

> **COLE**
> *(acting)*
> Ooh! Cold!

Amanda laughs.

> **AMANDA**
> *(acting)*
> Shall I pop it in the microwave for you?

The Script Supervisor, confused, consults her script. The Director smiles.

> **AMANDA**
> *(acting)*
> I hope you're enjoying your stay.

COLE
(acting)
Very much.

AMANDA
(acting)
Your manager called while you were
out.
As you thought he would, he asked me
not to tell you he called.

COLE
(acting)
What did you say?

AMANDA
(acting)
I told him you were upstairs strumming
your guitar at that very moment,
playing something festive-like.

Cole eats another bite.

AMANDA
(acting)
Then I think I heard him do one of
these...

She pumps her fist.

COLE
(acting)
I'm sure you heard right.

Amanda takes a scoop of her sundae.

AMANDA
(acting)
But, I didn't hear your guitar.

COLE
(acting)
Oh, so now you're checking on me?

Amanda raises an eyebrow.

COLE
(acting)
Two days after I leave here, I'm recording a live Christmas show with some other artists. I'll perform a few classics, but my manager thinks it's an opportunity to bring a new classic into the world.

AMANDA
(acting)
Which you haven't written yet.

COLE
(acting)
Which is why I'm here—where it snows —to set the mood.

He digs his spoon into his sundae.

COLE
(acting)
That was the plan anyway.

Amanda considers the problem, and then stands and picks up both of their sundaes. As she heads toward the kitchen...

AMANDA
(acting)
Get your jacket. I'm taking you on a
hunt for the Christmas spirit.

The kitchen door closes behind her.

DIRECTOR
Cut! Perfect.

Amanda returns, holding out one of the sundaes.

AMANDA
I'm sorry, Cole, did you want to finish
this?

COLE
Only if you have sour cream and chives
back there.

EXT. CHRISTMAS SHOPPE - DAY

Filming: *Decked in coats and scarves, Amanda and Cole walk down
a sidewalk. Cole also wears his cowboy hat. They pass a
SHOPKEEPER shoveling fake snow off the walk. His store window
is decorated with Christmas lights and snowflakes that twinkle.*

AMANDA
(acting)
Window shopping always puts me in
the spirit.

COLE
(acting)
Who are we buying for?

AMANDA
(acting)
No one.

In the street, the Camera Operator pushes a camera on tracks parallel to the actors. There is no snow beyond the curb or much further down the sidewalk than the store.

Amanda stops walking and the camera stops moving. She points at the shop window.

AMANDA
(acting)
Take this tin of caramel corn. My
handyman would love that. Even better
would be some homemade caramel
corn. So, I'll make him some!

COLE
(acting)
Are you saying I should write a song
about window shopping?

AMANDA
(acting)
Maybe. The point is to get your heart…

She places a hand on Cole's chest.

AMANDA
(acting)
…into the holiday spirit so you can

share it with your fans.

Cole looks down at her hand.

Amanda clears her throat and continues walking until she's out of shot.

DIRECTOR
Cut! Brilliant. Moving on.

Cole unwraps his scarf.

COLE
Summer does not go well with winter
clothes.

Amanda takes his hand and leads him toward the shop door.

AMANDA
Follow me.

INT. CHRISTMAS SHOPPE - DAY

A bell rings over the door as Amanda leads Cole inside. The interior is designed to look like a holiday gift shop.

AMANDA
We can stay in here where it's cool while
they set the next scene.

COLE
I will never underestimate actors in
scarves and sweaters again.

Amanda turns a snowglobe upside down.

AMANDA
So, it's harder than you thought?

The bell rings as the Script Supervisor pokes in her head.

SCRIPT SUPERVISOR
Just return everything where you found
it. We've got this all set up for
tomorrow.

Amanda sets down the snowglobe.

COLE
Serious question…

Amanda waits.

COLE
Will my fans buy me in this cowboy hat?
Do you think I pull it off?

AMANDA
Cole, how much of this guy is you?

COLE
Maybe seventy-percent. Eighty?

AMANDA
And the other twenty?

COLE
Well, the guy onscreen hasn't been in a
real relationship for six years.

Amanda pretends to be interested in looking at ornaments.

AMANDA
And how does that differ from the man
offscreen?

COLE
It's been five.

AMANDA
Why is that?

COLE
As you know, having a famous face
makes relationships hard to navigate.

AMANDA
Which is why I plan to look outside
Hollywood for my next one.

COLE
Oh. I see.

He approaches a rack of mistletoe.

COLE
Tell me, have you picked out our
mistletoe yet?

Amanda walks beside him.

AMANDA
That scene's not for a few more days.
And you don't get a say in it.

COLE
Excuse me? They're my lips, too.

He pulls off one of the mistletoe and hands it to her.

COLE
I think I'd like to kiss you under this
one.

Amanda is embarrassed.

COLE
You know, in an acting sort of way.

The bell above the door rings again. COLE'S MOM, mid-60s, enters.

COLE'S MOM
They told me you were in here!

Cole opens his arm and walks toward her.

COLE
Mom!

AMANDA
(to self)
Mom?

While hugging, Cole's Mom sees Amanda over his shoulder.

COLE'S MOM
And there she is!

Cole takes his mom to meet Amanda.

COLE
Mom, this is my co-star, Amanda Fox.

AMANDA
It is such an honor to meet you.

COLE'S MOM
Call me Sally. And it is an honor to meet you, too.

Cole points to the mistletoe Amanda holds.

COLE
Mom, that's the mistletoe I'm going to kiss her under.

COLE'S MOM
It's your high school dream come true.

Amanda looks at Cole.

AMANDA
I like your mom's honesty.

Commercial Break

ACT III

INT. FANCY RESTAURANT – NIGHT

Amanda, the Director, and the Elderly Man and Woman sit at a table drinking wine. There are two extra place settings.

DIRECTOR
You've done a number of these,
Amanda. With one day of filming left,
how do you think this went?

ELDERLY MAN
We've all done more than enough of
these.

AMANDA
This has gone smoother than most. And
all praise should go to the director.

The Director smiles.

ELDERLY WOMAN
Country boy really impressed me. And

48

he is adorable!
(to Amanda)
Were you nervous at first? I sure had my
concerns.

DIRECTOR
I'm sure we all did.

AMANDA
In all honesty, I think this could be a
second career for him.

The Director laughs.

DIRECTOR
If he's willing to play someone different
than himself.

AMANDA
Oh, this was a stretch for him. Cole
would never wear a cowboy hat.

Cole and his Mom are taken to their table by the MAITRE D'.

Cole gets his Mom seated before seating himself.

COLE
Can I say, the past couple weeks have
been some of the highlights of my
career.

ELDERLY MAN
Are you serious?

COLE'S MOM
He is being very serious.

49

ELDERLY MAN
Pretending you're freezing even though
it's hot out? A rushed production that
will never win you an Emmy?

ELDERLY WOMAN
You sure complain a lot.

DIRECTOR
I would swear you two were actually
married.

Cole points toward the elderly couple.

COLE
That's good acting.

ELDERLY WOMAN
And I definitely deserve an Emmy
nomination for it.

COLE
Yes, I loved the whole experience.

ELDERLY MAN
No screaming fans? No—

COLE
The same bed for days in a row.

COLE'S MOM
And I would be a fully contented
mother if these televised romances led
to actual romance.

The Elderly Woman looks expectantly from Cole's Mom to Cole.

COLE
We've talked this over plenty.
Being on the road—

COLE'S MOM
Being on the road makes things difficult.
I know.

COLE
Maybe when things slow down...

AMANDA
Really? Would you want things to slow
down that much?

Cole looks at Amanda briefly.

AMANDA
When the press stops following you,
that's when you know your star's begun
to fade.

ELDERLY WOMAN
What about you, Amanda? Are there—?

AMANDA
When I'm ready for something serious,
it will not be with someone in
entertainment—any version of it.

The Elderly Woman and Man look from Amanda to Cole.

COLE

You can put limits on your happiness
like that?

Everyone looks from Cole to Amanda.

AMANDA
Don't you?

COLE
On the timing, not the person.

AMANDA
Trust me, when you marry your co-star
like I did—

COLE'S MOM
That guy with the funny sideburns?

AMANDA
The press would not leave us alone.
But when you date a banker, a chef, or a
stay-at-home dad, then they pass right
on by.

COLE
No celebrities. Got it.

The WAITRESS arrives.

WAITRESS
Does everyone know what they want?

COLE
Apparently.

Cole and his Mom open their menus.

COLE
I'm going to need a minute.

The Waitress leaves.

ELDERLY WOMAN
(cheerful)
Imagine if you two started dating.
Especially after meeting on a romance!

AMANDA
Imagine.

Still perusing the menu...

COLE
If there's one thing these movies tell
you, your heart is the last thing you
should follow.

ELDERLY MAN
That is not what...
I thought you said you watched these
movies.

ELDERLY WOMAN
(whispering)
Irony. Look it up.

INT. FORGET-ME-NOT ANTIQUES - DAY

Filming: Cole hangs his cowboy hat on a rack and begins to browse. Holly, garland, and tinsel decorate the store for the holidays.

CUSTOMERS notice Cole and most struggle to not stare. He smirks while pretending to not notice.

A Customer tries to sneak a photo. Cole smiles and points as the camera flashes.

The Customer looks embarrassed.

> **COLE**
> *(acting)*
> It's okay. Just be sure to tag me.

The STORE OWNER, 70, approaches.

> **STORE OWNER**
> *(acting)*
> May I help you?

> **COLE**
> *(acting)*
> I'm looking for an old-fashioned portable radio.

> **STORE OWNER**
> *(acting)*
> Old-fashioned is what we do.

> **COLE**
> *(acting)*
> If it's got a big fat station dial on the front, that'd be the one I want.

> **STORE OWNER**
> *(acting)*

Follow me.

LATER

Filming: *A radio the size of a toaster is on the counter at the register. Cole extends the antennae way up.*

COLE
(acting)
Perfect!

STORE OWNER
(acting)
May I ask the story?

COLE
(acting)
The story?

STORE OWNER
(acting)
In this shop, every item has one story
coming in and gets another one going
out.

COLE
(acting)
That makes sense.
Well, I'm a country singer—

STORE OWNER
(acting)
I know who you are, silly.
I'm a fan, actually. Just wanted to give
you your space.

The two of them shake hands over the counter.

COLE
(acting)
Maybe I'm just nostalgic, but I recorded
a Christmas song recently and those
songs don't sound right until you hear
them coming through one of these.
That's how I heard them when I was a
child.

STORE OWNER
(acting)
Oh, you can't be that old.

The Store Owner pushes in the antennae.

COLE
(acting)
It's what we had.
So, that's the new story for this old
radio. Or, part of it.

The Store Owner begins to wrap the radio in packing paper.

STORE OWNER
(acting)
Then I hope your new song sounds like
your old memories.

The radio is placed in a bag on the counter. Cole lifts the bag and holds it under his arm.

STORE OWNER
(acting)

Merry Christmas.

COLE
(*acting*)
Merry Christmas.

Cole and the Store Owner smile at each other. They keep smiling.

Finally, Cole looks out of the corner of his eye toward...

DIRECTOR
Sorry. Cut!

Cole and the Store Owner relax.

INT. DRESSING ROOM - DAY

Amanda, on the middle stool, gets her make-up applied.

MAKE-UP ARTIST
When your show wraps, I've got to
clean this place up and move it to the
other side of town. Belinda's got a movie
starting next week.

AMANDA
For Christmas?

MAKE-UP ARTIST
'Tis the season.

AMANDA
Maybe I'll run over and say hi.

MAKE-UP ARTIST

You should do a cameo! It'd be a
Homeroom reunion.

AMANDA
And get in a catfight over who's
upstaging who? No thank you.
Oops. Did I say that out loud?

MAKE-UP ARTIST
What's said in the make-up chair stays
in the make-up chair.
So, today's the big day, right? The big
kiss?

AMANDA
Oh, is that today?

MAKE-UP ARTIST
What number is this for you?

AMANDA
Are we talking scripted kisses or in
total?

The door opens and Jessica and Natalie burst in.

*The Make-Up Artist rotates Amanda's chair toward the door but
continues working.*

AMANDA
What are you two—?

JESSICA
Road trip! Because we deserved it.

NATALIE

I called shotgun.

JESSICA
(to Natalie)
It was my car. No one was with us.

NATALIE
I still called it.

The Make-Up Artist turns Amanda back toward the mirror. Jessica and Natalie sit in the empty seats.

JESSICA
We wanted to take you out to celebrate another Christmas movie padding your resume.

AMANDA
Do they really pad, though?

NATALIE
We also know what you're filming today and wanted to see the fireworks ourselves.

MAKE-UP ARTIST
Oh? Are there fireworks?

JESSICA
There's a little sizzling.

AMANDA
(to Make-Up Artist)
And I never said that out loud to anyone, either.

JESSICA
You didn't have to.

NATALIE
We should do what we did in high school. "Excuse me, Cole? We were wondering if you liked our friend Amanda."

Amanda covers her face with her hands.

MAKE-UP ARTIST
Hands down. You're covering my canvas.

INT. BED & BREAKFAST / FOYER – NIGHT

Filming: *The doorbell rings. Amanda opens the door.*

On the doormat is a present (the size of a toaster) wrapped in Christmas paper. Amanda looks around but no one is there.

INT. BED & BREAKFAST / LIVING ROOM - NIGHT

Filming: *Amanda sets the present on the coffee table. She unwraps the old radio.*

A yellow Post-It note has a red arrow pointing to a location on the station bar and says "Tune in at 9:15pm."

Amanda looks at the grandfather clock: 9:05.

LATER

Filming: *The old radio, tuned to the arrow, plays a Christmas song with a female vocalist. Amanda sits on the couch, sipping a mug of hot chocolate with tiny marshmallows.*

She looks at the clock: 9:15.

> **RADIO DJ** *(from radio)*
> There's nothing better than a classic
> carol to get you in the Christmas spirit.
> But every so often a new song comes
> along and you just know it's a classic in
> the making.
> This next one sure has me in the spirit.
> Maybe it'll do the same for you.

Music for "Under the Mistletoe" begins.

> **RADIO DJ** *(from radio)*
> This one also comes as a request, going
> out to the beautiful bed-and-breakfast
> owner who inspired it.

Amanda nearly chokes on her drink.

> **COLE** *(from radio)*
> *(singing)*
> Oh, the mistletoe
> Is hanging low
> As the wind blows the treetops
> Dusted all with snow

Amanda covers her mouth with joy. This turns into a yearning for the musician she inspired.

> **COLE** *(from radio)*
> *(singing)*
> So come on, my dear
> Stand a little nearer

> Let's let our toes touch
> Under the mistletoe

The doorbell rings.

INT. BED & BREAKFAST / FOYER - NIGHT

Filming: *Amanda opens the door. It's Cole! And it's snowing.*

COLE *(from radio)*
(singing)
Under the mistletoe
Don't you know, in the snow
There ain't rules like we had in school

The song continues.

AMANDA
(acting)
What are you—?

COLE
(acting)
You inspire me.

He holds out his hand. Amanda gives her hand to him and steps outside.

EXT. BED & BREAKFAST / PORCH - NIGHT

Filming: *The song continues in the background.*

COLE
(acting)

I know the mistletoe can be used as just
an excuse...

AMANDA
(acting)
I love the song. And I love that you
wrote it in my home.

COLE
(acting)
With you in mind.

Out of the scene, just off the porch, Jessica and Natalie watch with tears in their eyes.

AMANDA
(acting)
I love mistletoe.

Cole nods.

AMANDA
(acting)
I wish I had some right now.

Cole smirks. Amanda looks up.

Mistletoe!

Cole puts his hands on her waist and Amanda closes her eyes. They kiss.

DIRECTOR
(to self)
I love this movie.

They keep kissing. The Crew watches.

Finally, the Camera Operator looks at the Director. The Director can't stop watching the kiss, so the Camera Operator taps her shoulder.

DIRECTOR
Oh. Cut!

The kiss continues.

DIRECTOR
Um… Cut?
Hello?

Cole opens one eye and looks from Amanda to the Director.

The Director smiles. Cole pulls back, still holding Amanda.

COLE
(to Director)
I'm sorry. I must not have heard you.

The Director raises her hands toward the crew.

DIRECTOR
That's a wrap!

The Crew all clap.

Amanda smiles at Cole.

AMANDA
I heard her say "Cut."

COLE
And yet you didn't pull away.

Amanda looks embarrassed.

AMANDA
I mean, I heard her the second time.

COLE
So…you knew she said it before?

Amanda is stumped. Cole likes this.

INT. DRESSING ROOM - NIGHT

Amanda sits in the middle chair and swipes through a tablet as the Make-Up Artist removes her make-up. She looks slightly annoyed.

Standing before another mirror in his cowboy hat, Cole mugs at his reflection.

COLE
I don't know, maybe it does fit me.

AMANDA
You'd better decide soon, you've got a
tour starting.
Things never slow down for Cole
Buskin.

Cole questions her tone and leans against the counter. Amanda turns her tablet so it faces him.

ON TABLET: A through-the-window photo at the Christmas Shoppe of Cole handing Amanda a mistletoe. Headline: "COUNTRY KISSES?"

AMANDA
According to the comments, there's a lot

of significance to us looking at this mistletoe.

COLE
On the bright side, people know about the movie.

AMANDA
On the only side, I now have to explain this to my son.

Cole looks apologetic.

AMANDA
Cole, I have loved getting to know you these past few weeks.

He waits on her words.

AMANDA
Who knows, maybe we can do it again.

COLE
Maybe we can…?

She looks toward the make-up counter, unable to face him.

AMANDA
But new characters. Maybe a sequel.

Cole takes off his hat and considers it.

COLE
Right.
Maybe I'll have my guy write us up a

new fake romance.

He sets his hat on the counter in front of Amanda.

COLE
I guess that is a wrap.

He leaves. The Make-Up Artist stops working and looks at Amanda's reflection in the mirror.

COMMERCIAL BREAK

ACT IV

INT. COOKING STUDIO - DAY

Filming: *At kitchenettes, TEAMS construct elaborate gingerbread houses. The COOKING INSTRUCTOR strolls between the houses, checking their progress.*

Belinda applies a gumdrop to a chimney with precision. She looks over the candy roof at MAX, mid-30s. He sets individual colored sprinkles along the eaves like Christmas lights.

BELINDA
(acting)
I'm done with my gumdrops. Do you
need help with your sprinkles?

Max takes his time with one more sprinkle, then looks up.

MAX
(acting)
I would love your help.

Belinda looks away, embarrassed.

Her expression turns serious as she spots someone off-camera. Concerned, DIRECTOR 2 follows Belinda's gaze.

Amanda, standing amongst the CREW, with Jessica (chewing gum) and Natalie, is the object of Belinda's concern.

DIRECTOR 2
Cut!

BELINDA
What is going on here?

Max sees Amanda, then lowers his eyes and shakes his head.

BELINDA
(to Director)
What's she doing here?

The Crew steps away from Amanda.

AMANDA
"She" is here to say hi.
Hi!

Belinda considers this, then fails at her attempt to smile.

DIRECTOR 2
Let's go to lunch, everyone.

Actors and Crew leave toward the food tables.

Max approaches Amanda and gives her a hug.

AMANDA
It's good to see you, Max.

MAX
(whispering)
To fall in love with her, I'm not a strong
enough actor.

Max leaves when Belinda approaches.

BELINDA
You're not here for a cameo or anything,
are you?

Amanda is at a loss for words.

BELINDA
I mean, a reunion would be huge! And
special. But it would take away from the
story we're trying to tell.

AMANDA
I'm not here to steal any thunder,
Belinda.

BELINDA
Good. I mean, I'm not afraid you would,
but...
Well, it is so good to see you!

She gives Amanda a hug. Jessica and Natalie look at each other, disgusted.

LATER

Amanda, Belinda, Jessica, and Natalie walk around the gingerbread houses, admiring them.

Belinda points out the house she was working on.

BELINDA
That one's real. The candy, the gingerbread, everything.

JESSICA
The rest of these are all fake? They look so—

BELINDA
Why, did you eat something? What are you chewing? You can't just eat movie props!

Jessica stops chewing her gum.

JESSICA
It's gum.

AMANDA
She was just impressed by how real they look.

Belinda maintains an untrusting glare at Jessica.

BELINDA
Okay. But that doesn't mean you can eat from the real one now that you know which one it is.

JESSICA
I—

BELINDA
Because that's the one Max and I fall in love over.

NATALIE
Just to be safe, we'll go hang out by the
real food.

*Belinda watches Jessica and Natalie leave. When they're a safe
distance away...*

BELINDA
You know, I was thinking about
stopping by your set, but...

Amanda waits.

AMANDA
But...?

BELINDA
But...I didn't

Amanda returns to admiring the gingerbread houses.

AMANDA
So, Belinda, what do you have lined up
when you finish here?

BELINDA
I'm doing a network pilot. Actually, Max
plays my neighbor in that, too.

Amanda looks at Max in the food line.

AMANDA
He would be great in a series.

BELINDA

Although, if it gets picked up, I'm going
to have to have a talk with him.
(*whispering*)
I think he's fallen for me.

Amanda struggles to maintain seriousness.

AMANDA
No, that wouldn't be good.

BELINDA
It's not like we're on *Homeroom*
anymore, right? We're not teenagers!
We have to be a little more responsible.

AMANDA
We weren't actually teenagers then.

BELINDA
In eight seasons, I think everyone pretty
much dated everyone.
I know I did.

AMANDA
That's true. Sometimes even before we
broke up.

BELINDA
Oh, bygones.
Tell me, what was it like working with a
musician?

AMANDA
Actually, he pulled it off.
(*looks around*)

Wait, is this *Gingerbread Home For the Holidays*?

BELINDA
Seriously?! Did they send you the script, too? They said I was the first person they offered it to!

AMANDA
No! I think I just saw it on the schedule.
(gestures around)
It's a fitting title.

Belinda doesn't believe her. Amanda feigns innocence.

BELINDA
Well, I don't know how you did it. I'd have a hard time pulling back from a kiss with that cowboy.

AMANDA
Honestly, it was not easy.

Belinda smiles.

BELINDA
Hold up. Was there a little unscripted romance on set?

AMANDA
No. I don't...
Of course not.

BELINDA
There was!

AMANDA
We were very professional. So even if
there was, no one said anything.

BELINDA
Since when does someone have to say
anything?
Are you going to pursue it?

AMANDA
No, that's—

BELINDA
Why not?

AMANDA
You know I won't put myself in another
situation like that.

BELINDA
Being with someone in the business?
You know what else is hard? Being with
someone who doesn't understand the
business.

AMANDA
Anyway…

BELINDA
You like him, Amanda. And if you let
that pass without seeing if it could work
this time, you will kick yourself forever.
That, I promise.

AMANDA

Are you giving me dating advice?

BELINDA
You know I'm right.
And you must really hate that.

EXT. TOUR BUS / TRUCK STOP 1 – NIGHT

Cole's bus is being filled with gas. Kristin exits the market and walks toward the bus.

INT. TOUR BUS - NIGHT

The curtains are shut and Christmas lights surround the windows. Cole reclines on a couch, eyes closed, listening to music through earbuds. Light-up snowflakes from the Christmas Shoppe set hang from the ceiling. Further back in the bus, Band Members play cards around a small table.

Kristin walks up from the front of the bus and sets a postcard of Missouri on Cole's lap. He opens his eyes and removes the earbuds.

COLE
A postcard?
Thanks, but I was here with you.

KRISTIN
Those are not so easy to find anymore.

COLE
Are you saying I need a hobby?
Collecting postcards from places I play?

KRISTIN

Well, you do need a hobby. All you've
talked about since the tour began is a
certain co-star from your previous job.

COLE
I have?

Kristin points to the decorations.

KRISTIN
And surrounding yourself with the
props to remind you.
She's not your co-star anymore, Cole.
You should call her.

COLE
She made herself perfectly clear. She
won't see anyone in showbiz.

KRISTIN
Fine. If you think you can stop thinking
about her...

Cole looks at the postcard.

COLE
So, what, just write and let her know I'm
thinking about her?

KRISTIN
That would make me feel special.

Kristin starts walking toward the front of the bus.

· · ·

EXT. TOUR BUS / TRUCK STOP 1 - NIGHT

Kristin exits the bus toward the market. A window slides open and Cole pokes his head out.

COLE
Done!

Kristin turns to him. He holds the postcard out the window.

COLE
Can you mail it for me?

Kristin reaches up and takes it from him.

KRISTIN
That was fast.

COLE
And straight to the point.

She looks at the postcard and smiles.

INT. AMANDA'S HOUSE / FOYER - NIGHT

The door swings open. Amanda lugs in several large luggage bags. Behind her, a taxi pulls away.

She gets the bags inside and closes the door.

PAUL *(off-screen)*
Honey? Are you home?

Amanda is confused, and then smiles with relief.

· · ·

INT. AMANDA'S HOUSE / KITCHEN - NIGHT

PAUL, late-30s, moviestar-looks, pours himself coffee.

Amanda sets her purse beside a large stack of mail. She begins to go through it.

PAUL
Patrick wanted to see you first thing in the morning.

AMANDA
Our boy is a sweetie.

PAUL
And rather than me getting up early to drive him, I thought I'd drop him off tonight and wait for you.

AMANDA
You're a great father, Paul.
And thanks for letting me tack on a few days. I shouldn't need to do anymore commercial work for the rest of the year.

PAUL
Cool. So, this Cole guy...

AMANDA
He's my co-star. That's it!
Why is everyone so—?

PAUL
You sure?

AMANDA

How do you even know to ask about
him?

PAUL
I was not being nosey…

She smirks: Of course not.

PAUL
But I brought in your mail and couldn't
help noticing three postcards from him.
All from different states.

She looks through the mail for the postcards.

AMANDA
He's on tour.

PAUL
And he wants you to know he's thinking
about you in every state he visits.

AMANDA
He did not say that.

PAUL
No, not in words.

Amanda finds the postcards. On the back of each is a drawing of a mistletoe.

PAUL
That's mistletoe, right?

Amused by her embarrassment, he takes a sip of coffee.

AMANDA
It's from a song. In our movie. That's
it.

PAUL
It's a kissy-kissy symbol is what it is.

AMANDA
Oh, who knows what it means.

PAUL
Anyway, I'm not a country music fan,
but while I waited up for you I watched
some of his videos.

AMANDA
What did you think? I like them!

PAUL
Eh.
I also read some of his interviews online.

AMANDA
But you're not nosey...

PAUL
Knowing how to spin an interview, I
also know how to read into them.

AMANDA
It's getting late...

Paul smiles and sets his coffee in the sink.

• • •

INT. AMANDA'S HOUSE / FOYER - NIGHT

Paul opens the door. He turns to Amanda.

> **PAUL**
> Tell Patrick I love him. We had a great
> time.

Amanda gives him a hug.

> **PAUL**
> And this Cole guy... He seems alright.
> I approve.

She playfully shoves him out the door.

> **AMANDA**
> He's my co-star.

INT. AMANDA'S HOUSE / OFFICE - NIGHT

Amanda looks at the framed DVDs and mistletoe. She sets the mistletoe from A Christmas Single *on her desk.*

In her back pocket, Amanda's phone rings with the melody from "Under the Mistletoe."

Excited, she takes a breath and then pulls out the phone.

EXT. TRUCK STOP 2 - NIGHT

Cole, on his phone, stands several feet from his tour bus. Band Members exit the bus toward the market.

> **COLE**

I hope it's not too late to call.

INTERCUT: TRUCK STOP & AMANDA'S HOUSE / OFFICE

AMANDA
I actually got back home not too long
ago.

COLE
Then you've seen that I've been thinking
of you.

AMANDA
Mistletoe, huh?

COLE
Look, if it—

AMANDA
Thank you.

COLE
I'm mailing them from the road because
...that's where I am. But I'm calling
because I'm playing near you this
weekend. About an hour away.

Amanda smiles.

COLE
And I would love it if you came as my
guest.

But then she shuts her eyes.

AMANDA
I've been gone awhile, Cole. My son—

COLE
Bring him with you! I'd love to meet him.

Amanda considers.

Commercial Break

ACT V

INT. FANCY HOTEL / LOBBY - DAY

Amanda checks in at the front desk. Patrick is behind her near the luggage.

AMANDA
Checking in for Amanda Fox.

Amanda sets her credit card and driver's license on the counter while the HOTEL CLERK types at the computer.

HOTEL CLERK
It looks like everything's been paid for,
Ms. Fox.

Amanda looks back at Patrick. Patrick looks impressed.

AMANDA
(to Hotel Clerk)
If you could please take the charges off
whatever card they're on and—

The Hotel Clerk reads from the screen.

HOTEL CLERK
"Do not let Ms. Fox pay for anything."

AMANDA
That is very nice, but—

HOTEL CLERK
"And don't listen to any excuses."

Amanda gives in and takes her cards.

MISS HEARTBREAKER *(off-screen)*
Amanda Fox?

Amanda's expression drops at the sight of Miss Heartbreaker.

MISS HEARTBREAKER
Isn't this the same hotel where Cole
Buskin is staying?

PATRICK
We're his guests!

Miss Heartbreaker tilts her head at Patrick.

MISS HEARTBREAKER
I have a son just about your age.

AMANDA
He must be so proud.

MISS HEARTBREAKER
As should your son, watching his mom

make a living.

AMANDA
Please excuse us. We're here to see a
show.

She holds Patrick close and walks away.

MISS HEARTBREAKER
(to self)
As am I.

INT. FANCY HOTEL / HALLWAY - DAY

Amanda and Patrick roll their luggage down the hall.

PATRICK
Something is obviously going on with
you and Cole.

AMANDA
Well, you are obviously wrong. We're
just—

PATRICK
I am not wrong.

AMANDA
Oh, brother. I should have booked you a
separate room.

INT. CONCERT HALL / STAGE - NIGHT

Cole and his Band play a slow song: "Uh Oh, Beautiful."

COLE
(singing)
We know we shouldn't go there
So we pretend we don't care
What the other feels
The sunshine starts to creep in
We feel our story begin
'Til we both sing along

The crowd sings along with the chorus.

COLE
(singing)
Uh-oh, it's a beautiful day
Uh-oh, it's a beautiful day
Uh-oh, it's a beautiful day
Oh, uh-oh, so beautiful

INT. CONCERT HALL / SIDESTAGE - NIGHT

Amanda and Patrick watch from the wings. Kristin watches from behind them.

COLE *(off-screen)*
(singing)
My breath it quickens
The drama thickens
I must hold on tight to what is right
What a fight

INT. CONCERT HALL / STAGE - NIGHT

They play the final chorus...

COLE
(singing)
Uh-oh, it's a beautiful day
Uh-oh, it's a beautiful day
Uh-oh, it's a beautiful day
Oh, uh-oh, you're beautiful

At the sustained final chord, the crowd cheers.

INT. CONCERT HALL / SIDESTAGE - NIGHT

AMANDA
I haven't heard that one before.
I like it!

Kristin is about to speak...

PATRICK
It's his new single. It already hit number
one!

AMANDA
Excuse me? Since when do you know so
much about country music?

PATRICK
Please don't tell my friends.

INT. CONCERT HALL / STAGE - NIGHT

COLE

Thank you! Glad you like it.
In fact, seems a whole lot of you are
liking it, streaming it, downloading it...

The crowd responds with more cheers.

COLE

Speaking of beautiful things, how many
of you know I recently finished filing
my first movie?

Cheers.

INT. CONCERT HALL / SIDESTAGE - NIGHT

Patrick looks up at Amanda. She stares nervously at the stage.

INTERCUT: CONCERT HALL / STAGE / SIDESTAGE

COLE

It's called *A Christmas Single* and
contains a brand new song by yours
truly.
How many of y'all would like to hear it
right now?

Huge cheers.

COLE

Well, alright. It's never too early for
Christmas!

The DRUMMER puts on a Santa hat. The other Band Members put on reindeer antlers.

COLE
And if you don't mind, I'd like to invite
my co-star on *A Christmas Single* to
the stage.
(to Amanda)
Bring yourself on out here!

Amanda shakes her head. Patrick applauds loudly.

COLE
It'd be a shame to do this without you
beside me.

Amanda starts walking onto the stage.

COLE
Ms. Amanda Fox, everyone!

The crowd roars.

Amanda sees a large sparkling mistletoe descending over the stage. She quickly returns for Patrick's hand and pulls him out with her.

COLE
And you must be Patrick! It is truly an
honor.

Cole shakes Patrick's hand.

COLE
Oh! One thing I forgot.

The Roadie runs onto the stage and puts a red cowboy hat with white fur trim on Cole's head.

COLE
Now that feels much better.

The Band begins to play "Under the Mistletoe."

COLE
(singing)
Oh, the mistletoe
Is hanging low
As the wind blows the treetops
Dusted all with snow

Amanda looks out at the screaming audience

AMANDA'S PERSPECTIVE: The sound is muted. Audience members hold up cameras. All movement slows and tilts.

Cole strums the last chord: sound and visuals return to normal.

COLE
Now, who's feeling that holiday spirit?

The crowd responds with cheers.

COLE
Go on, share some of that mistletoe
cheer with whoever you're near!

Cole looks at Amanda.

She looks at the crowd: Several people kiss. Even more cameras are raised!

She looks up at the mistletoe.

Cole smiles at her and raises his eyebrows.

Amanda kisses Patrick on the forehead. Then she grabs his hand and rushes offstage.

Passing Kristin...

AMANDA
Tell him we left for the hotel. We're checking out.

INT. FANCY HOTEL / ROOM - NIGHT

Amanda and Patrick fold clothes and put them into suitcases on their beds.

PATRICK
All I'm saying is, he obviously thought something was going on.

AMANDA
And he knew enough about me to know that was not the way to show it.

A knock at the door. Patrick walks over to answer it.

AMANDA
If they're here for the luggage, it'll be a minute.

Patrick returns with Cole, still in his sweaty concert clothes.

COLE
Amanda, I know I did something, but I have no idea what.

Amanda keeps packing.

AMANDA
How many of your fans had phones out
recording us? By now, we could be
uploaded and circling the world over
and over—

COLE
For a song? It's a good song, I know,
but—

AMANDA
For a kiss!

COLE
A what?!

AMANDA
You raised your eyebrows at me!
And the mistletoe?

PATRICK
Should I leave? Or maybe I'll go to the
bathroom.

AMANDA
No.

COLE
Dude, if you need to go...

AMANDA
Cole, I am proud of the movie we made.
I can't wait for people to see it. But if

you did this to guarantee ratings, then I
can guarantee—

COLE
Whoah! Over my eyebrows?

Patrick walks toward the bathroom.

PATRICK
Yep. I'm going to the bathroom.

He shuts the door behind him.

COLE
If I raised my eyebrows, it was because
of their reaction. They were really
excited!

Amanda doesn't believe him.

COLE
Sometimes I raise them before I sneeze,
too. What do you want me to say?

AMANDA
Miss Heartbreaker was probably there.
Did you know that?

COLE
I did an interview with her.

AMANDA
You knew she was there?!

COLE

I'm an entertainer! That's how I make
my living.

AMANDA
And she makes hers talking about
people like you and me.
Did she ask about me?

COLE
What would there be to say?

Awkward pause.

COLE
Amanda, I wanted you and Patrick to
come to my show. That's it.

She wants to believe him.

AMANDA
You're saying you wouldn't have
wanted to kiss me onstage?

COLE
Well, it would guarantee better ratings…
I'm kidding!

AMANDA
Because that is not how I want us to
start a relationship.

He pauses. Did she just say…?

COLE
Okay. So how would…?

Amanda realizes what she said. She turns toward her suitcase and Patrick reenters the room.

PATRICK
I didn't really have to go.

Amanda closes the lid on her suitcase even though not everything is packed.

AMANDA
You don't have to pack any more.
We'll leave in the morning.
(to Cole)
I appreciate you clarifying things.

COLE
Did we clarify things?

AMANDA
I think so.
Good night, Cole.

He backs toward the door.

COLE
I really am glad you both were there.

He exits.

PATRICK
Nope, nothing going on there.

Commercial Break

ACT VI

INT. CABIN - DAY

In a small rustic cabin decorated for Christmas, including a lit gingerbread candle, Cole sits on the edge of a couch. One heel taps impatiently as he gazes at his acoustic guitar in a stand a few feet away. At his feet, a notebook is shut with a pen on top.

About to push himself toward the guitar...

He collapses back on the couch, defeated. He puts his head in his hands. Outside (off-screen), tires roll over gravel.

EXT. CABIN - DAY

The ground is covered in snow. Kristin walks up the semi-cleared steps to the front porch.

She knocks on the door.

INT. CABIN - DAY

Cole pours coffee into a mug and hands it to Kristin.

COLE
Black, right?

She accepts the mug and takes a sip.

Cole pours coffee into another mug. Into his, he pours creamer until the black coffee is light brown.

KRISTIN
Let me guess, you forgot to grab
Cinnamon Roll creamer on your way up
here.

COLE
If you go to town, will you grab some?

KRISTIN
For some reason, I don't picture Hank
Williams needing his coffee to taste like
a snickerdoodle.

Cole sits on the couch. Kristin sits on a nearby chair.

KRISTIN
I'm here. What's going on, Cole?

Cole opens his arms.

COLE
I can't write!

KRISTIN
This has been your songwriting
sanctuary for the past two albums.
You haven't written anything?

COLE
I've been writing, but none of it works.

Kristin takes a sip, waiting for him to continue.

COLE
My audience should see themselves in
my songs, or be able to picture who they
love.
That's always been my philosophy.

Cole picks up his notebook and flips it open.

COLE
These lyrics are way too specific.
They're all about...

He looks at Kristin.

KRISTIN
Get out!

She takes the notebook and Cole puts his head in his hands.

INT. AMANDA'S HOUSE / FOYER - DAY

Amanda opens the door. Owen is outside in a warm coat and carrying a cardboard box full of scripts.

AMANDA
Thanks for bringing those over.

She steps aside and Owen walks in.

OWEN

This isn't like you. Am I right to be
concerned?

She closes the door behind him.

INT. AMANDA'S HOUSE / KITCHEN - DAY

*Owen carries the box to the island counter and sets it down. He
takes her hands and looks her in the eyes.*

OWEN
Are you having money concerns?

AMANDA
Who isn't?

OWEN
Do you owe money? Is someone coming
after you to collect?

AMANDA
I just want to do a movie. Something for
me.

OWEN
I'm not buying it.
When you hired me, you gave me very
specific instructions. With *Homeroom*
in heavy syndication, you would do
three commercials and one movie a year.
That's it. The rest of your time went to
Patrick, friends, and volunteering.

AMANDA
And now I'm an actor who wants to act

more.

Amanda pulls out a script and flips to the first page. Owen studies her carefully.

OWEN
Nope. Not buying it.

Patrick enters with a large plastic tub full of tinsel and garland.

PATRICK
Hi, Owen. Mom, should I put this in the
living room?

OWEN
About to start Christmasing the place
up?

AMANDA
We're getting the tree later today.

PATRICK
You should come!

OWEN
How about you two get the tree and I'll
help you decorate it?

Patrick leaves with the decorations. Owen pulls the box of scripts closer to him.

OWEN
I'll stay and look through these.

Amanda lifts a coat from a stool and begins to put it on.

AMANDA
Find me something good.
If it starts filming soon, even better.

OWEN
This isn't a movie you're looking for. I
think you want to disappear into any
role other than Amanda Fox right now.
Am I right?

AMANDA
I'm getting a tree.

She leaves him alone in the kitchen.

INT. CABIN - DAY

Cole reclines on the couch, an arm draped across his forehead. Kristin sits on a chair, reading pages in his notebook.

KRISTIN
I mean, this wouldn't be so bad if it were
a concept album.

She flips another page.

KRISTIN
You've got one song about her eyes.

COLE
Getting lost in them.

She keeps flipping pages.

KRISTIN

One about her laugh. The way she smells. Her walk.

She turns one last page.

KRISTIN
And one more about her eyes.

COLE
Finding my way home in them.

He sits up.

COLE
I'm a mess!

KRISTIN
You are a mess.

COLE
What do I do? Call the album *Amanda*?

KRISTIN
You need to see her, Cole. If you don't see her, you'll never stop thinking about her.

COLE
I don't know if that makes sense.

KRISTIN
You need to see her so you can stop obsessing about not seeing her.

Cole considers this.

KRISTIN
I do kind of love it, though.
The woman who played the inspiration
for a fictional Cole upsets the creativity
of the real Cole.

COLE
My mom cannot know about this.

KRISTIN
Definitely not.

INT. AMANDA'S HOUSE / LIVING ROOM - NIGHT

A Christmas tree is set in the corner. Its strands of colored lights are lit throughout the branches. Amanda, Patrick, and Owen hang ornaments that have been set out on the coffeetable.

OWEN
Growing up, my family always used
white lights.

PATRICK
I like white lights.

AMANDA
I always felt they looked stuffy. Like the
people were too cool for color.
No offense.

OWEN
Offense taken.

AMANDA
My porch light is white. Street lights are
white.
Christmas should be colorful!

OWEN
We're all creatures of habit, I guess.

*Amanda watches the playful interaction between Patrick and Owen,
letting each other admire the next ornament before they hang it.*

*Her joy turns to wistful longing. She looks through the remaining
ornaments and picks up an elf playing an acoustic guitar.*

She stares at it as Patrick and Owen continue decorating.

EXT. CABIN - NIGHT

Cole walks Kristin down the steps to her car.

COLE
Thanks for coming all this way just to
tell me I've got it bad.

KRISTIN
You pay me for the truth.

She opens her car door and gets in, but before shutting it…

KRISTIN
I have to make some calls to set it in
stone, but there's a morning show doing
a series on the annual onslaught of
Christmas romance movies.
As a musician turned-actor, they'd love
to interview you and have you play the

new song.

COLE
Just let me know when and where.

Kristin shuts her door and starts the engine.

Cole watches the car back down the road. Then he considers a possibility.

COLE
Wait!

Kristin lowers the driver's side window as Cole walks up.

COLE
This morning show, are they only
interested in me? Or can I bring
someone along?

Kristin smiles.

KRISTIN
They only inquired about you.

COLE
Ask them to inquire again.

Kristin shakes her head as her window goes up.

COLE
Drive safe.

She continues backing down the road and Cole walks back toward the cabin.

. . .

INT. AMANDA'S HOUSE / LIVING ROOM - NIGHT

The tree is decorated except for the angel on top.

AMANDA
There's only one thing missing.
Patrick?

Owen picks up the angel and holds it out for Patrick.

PATRICK
Can you get me a chair?

Patrick holds onto the angel as Owen lifts him up.

OWEN
This is way faster!

As Patrick places the angel gently on top of the tree...

AMANDA
Make a wish, everyone.

Setting Patrick down, Owen's phone beeps.

He pulls out his phone, reads the text, and smiles.

AMANDA
What is it?

OWEN
First, tell me what you wished for.

Commercial Break

ACT VII

INT. MORNING SHOW / SET - DAY

Filming: *The HOST sits in a chair facing a camera. Behind her, a cartoon sun in a Santa hat hangs over a city skyline.*

HOST
If you're like me, you look forward to so many things this time of year, including the return of Christmas romance movies. Several channels now do a month-long countdown with a different movie every night. Many are repeats, but every year a new slate of stories covered in tinsel and snow are added to the roster.
We're lucky to have the two stars of the forthcoming *A Christmas Single* with us today, Amanda Fox and Cole Buskin.

Amanda and Cole sit in chairs angled toward the Host. Behind their chairs is a decorated Christmas tree.

HOST

Amanda, many of us got to know you as
the sweet but naive new student on
Homeroom. But for the past several
years you've been a staple on these
holiday love stories.

AMANDA

To be honest, I'm a fool for anything
Christmas.

HOST

Tell me a little about this year's movie.

AMANDA

Well, it's about a country musician…
(gestures toward Cole)
…wanting to write a Christmas song.
But he lives in Texas, so he rents a room
at a snowy bed-and-breakfast in the
northeast to get inspired.

HOST

And you play…?

AMANDA

I run the bed-and-breakfast.

HOST

And romance ensues, I'm guessing.
Now, Cole, you've been burning up the
country charts. What made you want to
do a TV movie?

COLE

Not just any TV movie. A Christmas romance!
And, as you can tell, this role was basically made for me.

HOST
It sure sounds like it.
Let's not forget to remind our audience that *A Christmas Single* debuts this Saturday night.
I have to ask, will you be watching?

COLE
Of course! Every Christmas season, my momma and I put mini-marshmallows in our hot cocoa, turn on the TV, and are reminded what this time of year is all about.

HOST
Amanda? Will you be watching?

AMANDA
My parents live in northern California and we get together every year to watch my new movie.
Well, most of it. I head to the other room when the kissing scene comes on.
I can't watch that with my parents!

HOST
What about you Cole? Will you stay for the kissing scene?

COLE

And then I'll probably rewind and
watch it again!

The Host laughs. Amanda playfully shoves Cole's shoulder.

HOST
Sounds like you really enjoyed shooting
your first romance.

COLE
I got to wear a cowboy hat and
everything.

The Host is confused but Amanda laughs.

HOST
Let's roll a clip.

INT. MORNING SHOW / CONTROL ROOM - DAY

A screen-bank displays varying angles of the main set as well as sets not in use. The PRODUCER looks at the "live" screen of Amanda and Cole. A graphic beneath them has their names and A CHRISTMAS SINGLE.

PRODUCER
These two look great together.

An ENGINEER hits a button. On the screen, Amanda and Cole are replaced by the logo for A Christmas Single.

INT. BED & BREAKFAST / DINING ROOM - DAY [ON TV]

Standing near the kitchen door, Amanda happily looks around her dining room table: two ELDERLY COUPLES, a YOUNG COUPLE, and a CHILD. Through the large window, it looks like summer outside.

> **NARRATOR** *(voiceover)*
> She runs a successful bed-and-breakfast;
> full every spring, summer, and fall.

INT. CONCERT STAGE - NIGHT [ON TV]

Cole, in a cowboy hat, plays his guitar and sings.

> **NARRATOR** *(voiceover)*
> He's a country music sensation hoping
> to write a hit Christmas single...

EXT. BED & BREAKFAST / PORCH - NIGHT [ON TV]

In the cowboy hat, holding his guitar case, Cole stands in the snow below the steps. He looks up at the falling snow.

> **NARRATOR** *(voiceover)*
> ...seeking inspiration in a town known
> for its holiday cheer.

At the dining room window, the curtains part. Amanda gazes out at Cole.

> **NARRATOR** *(voiceover)*
> And there is one more room at the inn
> tonight...

Close on Amanda.

> **NARRATOR** *(voiceover)*
> ...along with plenty of inspiration.

Fade out.

INT. MORNING SHOW / SET - DAY

> **HOST**
> I can tell those two will end up together!

> **AMANDA**
> It wouldn't be a Christmas romance if
> they didn't.

> **COLE**
> That's why I love these. It's not about
> will they, but how will they and why.

> **HOST**
> I never thought of it that way.

> **COLE**
> What roads will they travel to bring
> them together? When will they notice
> the person right beside them?

Amanda and the Host look surprised at his TV romance philosophy.

> **COLE**
> I spend a lot of alone time on the road.

> **HOST**

(to camera)
When we come back, Cole Buskin
performs his brand new song, "Under
the Mistletoe."

The Host leans forward and shakes hands with her guests.

HOST
You can take off your mics now.
Thank you both so much! It was a real
pleasure.
Cole, they're ready for you next door.

*Amanda and Cole remove their microphones. The MAKE-UP
CREW rushes in to touch-up the Host's face.*

HOST
Do you two have plans while you're
here, or do you fly your separate ways
after this?

AMANDA
(to Cole)
I think we're both staying until the
morning, right?

COLE
Maybe we can get in some Christmas
shopping. This is a much bigger city
than where I live.

AMANDA
Sounds fun. I'm in.

HOST

Not waiting 'til the last minute. Smart.

EXT. BETTY'S ANTIQUES - DAY

The glass door is frosted with fake snow. Jingle bells hang on the push bar. A sheet of paper taped to the glass shows a camera with a line through it: "ABSOLUTELY NO PHOTOGRAPHY INSIDE."

INT. BETTY'S ANTIQUES - DAY

A Christmas tree in the middle of the store has small items attached to it with price tags: stuffed animals, CD cases, ornaments...

Amanda and Cole walk around the tree, touching different items.

AMANDA
I love this!

COLE
If you want unique gifts, start in an antique store.

AMANDA
Our movie is much more you than I anticipated.

Amanda notices a customer watching them.

Cole turns toward where she was looking.

COLE
They might look, but you'll notice they aren't taking pictures.

AMANDA
Only because of that sign on the door.

COLE
I stopped by earlier and asked them to
put that up.

AMANDA
Wait. You planned on coming here?

COLE
But if I planned on coming alone, I
wouldn't have done that.

Amanda stares at him as Cole removes a CD case from the tree.

COLE
This! Dolly and Kenny's *Once Upon a
Christmas*. This right here is Christmas!

AMANDA
I remember watching that special when I
was a kid.

COLE
Would you mind if I bought it for
Patrick?

AMANDA
Not at all.

COLE
If you give it to him now, you can both
listen to it as you countdown to our
show.

She carefully takes the CD from him and looks at it.

COLE
Is that weird?

AMANDA
Of course not. This album obviously
means a lot to you.

COLE
I was around his age when I first heard
it. And I probably didn't stop listening
until Valentine's Day.

AMANDA
They sure made quite a duo.
Patrick will love it.

She offers him back the CD.

COLE
Without Christmas music, or movies
about Christmas music, I may never
have met his mother.

Amanda smiles.

LATER

Cole and Amanda are in different parts of the store. Cole peruses old vinyl records.

Amanda looks through shelves of DVDs and VHS tapes. Something catches her eye. She looks across the store to Cole, and then laughs as she removes something from the shelf.

Cole flips through records. Into his field of vision, Amanda puts a

VHS tape of Homeroom. *Her younger self is on the cover in once-trendy teen clothes.*

COLE
No way!

He takes it from her.

AMANDA
I don't know if your mom still has a way to play these, but—

COLE
She does!

AMANDA
That includes the season one Christmas episode, which is when our show began to take off.

COLE
She'll love it. Thank you.

AMANDA
Without it, I may never have met her son.

He looks at her.

COLE
Okay, but I'm definitely watching it before I give it to her.

AMANDA
Of course.

INT. HOTEL / HALLWAY - NIGHT

The hallway lights are ringed with Christmas wreaths. Amanda and Cole each carry two shopping bags full of gifts, wrapped and unwrapped. They stop at a door and Amanda sets down her bags.

She pulls a room key from her pocket and unlocks the door. She holds the door open with her back while looking at Cole.

AMANDA
Well, thank you for today.

COLE
Thank you for dinner. You really didn't
have to pay.

AMANDA
I chose the place and it was horrible.
That was my penance.

They lock eyes for a long time.

COLE
So...

Amanda unfreezes her gaze and picks up her bags.

AMANDA
Goodnight, Cole.

Cole nods.

COLE
Right. I do have an elevator to catch.

Goodnight, Amanda.

She closes the door behind her. Cole exhales.

INT. HOTEL / AMANDA'S ROOM - NIGHT

Amanda lays on her bed, staring up. She's fully clothed, including shoes. The bags of gifts are undisturbed at the foot of the bed.

She looks over at the phone and contemplates.

INT. HOTEL / RESTAURANT - NIGHT

Elevator doors open. Cole steps out, dressed the same as we last saw him.

He walks into a nearly empty, but festively decorated, restaurant.

Amanda, at a small table, smiles as she sees him.

COLE
And dessert to top off a wonderful day.

Standing beside Amanda's table, he offers his open hand.

COLE
But do you mind if we move further
back? I don't want anyone to spot us.

She takes his hand and they walk toward a more private area.

AMANDA
Oh, but wouldn't having our picture
taken help the ratings?

He smirks and they sit at a small table.

AMANDA
I hope you don't mind, but I already
ordered for both of us.

COLE
And paid for dinner?
I feel a little emasculated, but…I like it!

Amanda looks down, avoiding his eyes.

AMANDA
Cole… I couldn't fall asleep thinking I
may not see you—

*A WAITER sets down two cups of vanilla ice cream with cherries
on top.*

COLE
(to Waiter)
Thank you. These look great.

Amanda digs in. Lifting the spoon to her mouth…

COLE
Wait, you can't eat yet. Let's get back to
what you were saying. Something about
not seeing me…

AMANDA
Hmm. I don't remember.

COLE
Maybe you couldn't fall asleep thinking
you may not see me… Pass my driver's
test?

Amanda laughs.

COLE
No, I already passed that.

She points her spoon at Cole's bowl.

AMANDA
Eat up. This ice cream melts.

As he pokes his spoon into the ice cream...

COLE
Then let me say that I will absolutely
miss you.

They look at each other in silence as they each finish a bite.

COLE
Let me ask you, because I don't read
Hollywood gossip sites. But I assume
you mostly dated other actors before
marrying one.

Amanda nods.

COLE
I see how that could get tiring. Actors
always pretending to be someone
they're not.

AMANDA
Mr. Cole, may I remind you that you are
now an actor, too.

COLE
But my focus is still music. I told my
manager I won't do more than one
movie a year, feature or TV.

AMANDA
My agreement is similar.

COLE
Because your focus is your boy.

AMANDA
Among other things, but he's at the top.

COLE
Where he should remain.

AMANDA
Thank you. I agree.

COLE
Which would be frustrating with the
paparazzi buzzing about.

AMANDA
Which would happen more than it
already does if I dated—

COLE
Me.

Amanda takes another bite.

COLE
Being famous is fun, I suppose, when

there's no one you need to protect.
And Patrick is worth protecting.

Amanda nods gently.

COLE
With the careers we both chose, we'll
always struggle for privacy.

He lifts a spoon of ice cream, but before he brings it to his mouth...

COLE
When I find someone whose heart is
worth that struggle, I hope she thinks
my heart is worth it, too.

AMANDA
Have you ever found someone worth
that?

COLE
Just recently.

Amanda picks up a spoon of ice cream, but only looks at it.

AMANDA
Like I said earlier, Patrick and I go to my
parents' to watch my movie every year.

COLE
And each year, my mom and I watch
your movie together.

AMANDA
I would love it if you and your mom

would come watch it with us.

INT. HOTEL / ELEVATOR - NIGHT

Amanda and Cole enter the elevator, both so happy.

As the doors almost close, an arm reaches in and stops it. They reopen to...

MISS HEARTBREAKER
Oh, you have got to be kidding me.
I have been hunting all over town for
you two!

She steps in and the doors close behind her. Cole presses two buttons.

COLE
We're on separate floors, Miss
Heartbreaker. That's not a story.

MISS HEARTBREAKER
Can I at least get one shot of you two in
here? No innuendo, I promise. There's
not even a mistletoe around this time.

The doors open. Reluctantly, Cole steps out.

COLE
(to Amanda)
You alright?

Amanda nods.

The doors close. Amanda and Miss Heartbreaker ride a few floors in silence.

AMANDA

We may disagree that acting and...
photojournalism...are equally serious
jobs. But you are a mother. Do you agree
that that is the most serious job?

Miss Heartbreaker looks down.

AMANDA

Good. Then I want to make a deal.

Commercial Break

ACT VIII

INT. PARENTS' HOUSE / DINING ROOM - NIGHT

*Amanda, with Jessica, Natalie, and BOYFRIEND 1 and 2, set the
table, which has a Christmas tablecloth. Christmas music plays on a
radio in a nearby room.*

JESSICA
What time is he supposed to be here?

AMANDA
He knows what time we're eating, but
they have to get through airport traffic
first.

BOYFRIEND 1
They?

BOYFRIEND 2
He's bringing his mom.

BOYFRIEND 1
(to Amanda)

Seriously?

JESSICA
He's a country boy. Take notes.

AMANDA'S MOM and DAD enter, each setting a red candlestick in the middle of the table. Her Mom lights them both.

"Under the Mistletoe" begins to play on the radio.

AMANDA'S MOM
Honey, that's the song from your movie.
Do you want me to turn it up?

AMANDA
That's okay, Mom.

JESSICA
This isn't even a country station. That
song is playing everywhere!

AMANDA
It's a good song.

NATALIE
It's a good song about you.

AMANDA
About a character.

NATALIE
Oh, honey, the movie was written for
you and so was the song.

AMANDA
The song was written before he met me.

JESSICA
It wasn't, actually. On our road trip to
watch you film, we brought along the
original script to read.

NATALIE
There were no lyrics in it.

AMANDA
What?

JESSICA
Maybe there were lyrics in the draft
used on set, but when you signed on, it
said—

NATALIE
"Lyrics to be added."

Amanda is confused.

AMANDA
I think you're right.

NATALIE
When he flew to your house to convince
you—

JESSICA
And I had to let him in because you
thought he was an autograph-hound.

NATALIE
You asked him to follow you to…

AMANDA
My office!

BOYFRIEND 1
Hey! That's where you keep the mistletoe from your movies.

NATALIE
(singing)
Let's let our toes touch
Under the mistletoe

AMANDA
Okay, okay, okay.

The music on the radio turns to talking.

BOYFRIEND 2
This guy is good.

AMANDA'S MOM *(off-screen)*
Honey, now they've got Cole on the phone!

INT. PARENTS' HOUSE / FAMILY ROOM - NIGHT

The Christmas tree is decorated and lit with colored lights. Three stockings hang on the mantle.

Jessica and Natalie run in from the kitchen, followed by their Boyfriends and Amanda. With Amanda's Mom and Dad, everyone stares at the radio.

COLE *(from radio)*

Oh, it's been wonderful! A song and a
movie? Maybe I should've written a
Christmas novel, too.

ANNOUNCER *(from radio)*
What I want to know is, will you be
watching the movie tonight, or would
that be too awkward?
I know I can't listen to tapes of my own
show.

COLE *(from radio)*
I'll be watching.
How else will I know if I made a fool of
myself and should stick to the guitar?

ANNOUNCER *(from radio)*
Well, I think everyone hearing you right
now is pulling for you.

Everyone looks at Amanda. She's smiling at his responses.

ANNOUNCER *(from radio)*
Where will you be watching it, Cole?
Someplace special?

Amanda is nervous.

COLE *(from radio)*
Of course. It's a special night.

Amanda bites her nails.

COLE *(from radio)*
My momma and I have a tradition of

watching these movies together,
whether I'm in them or not.
That's not a tradition I want to break.

Amanda sighs and smiles.

ANNOUNCER *(from radio)*
Thank you for joining us, Cole.
And there you have it! He'll be watching
right along with all of you.
Watching it with his momma.

Jessica, heartbroken, lays her head on Amanda's shoulder.

JESSICA
He's not coming?
Boys are such jerks.
And now that includes country boys,
too.

NATALIE
No, he's just not making a spectacle.
He'll be here.

Jessica looks at Amanda: Is that right? Amanda nods.

JESSICA
Oh. Then don't tell him what I said
about country boys.

INT. PARENTS' HOUSE / FOYER - NIGHT

A knock at the door. Amanda's Mom and Dad open it.

Cole and his Mom are bundled in scarves, coats, and mittens because there's real snow outside.

AMANDA'S MOM
You must be Cole!
We're so glad you made it.

COLE
This is my mom, Sally.

COLE'S MOM
Thank you so much for inviting me.

AMANDA'S MOM
Of course! Come in.

Cole and Amanda's Dad shake hands.

AMANDA'S MOM
I hope the traffic wasn't too bad.

COLE
It gave me time to do a radio call-in.

AMANDA'S MOM
We heard!

Jessica looks embarrassed.

Patrick squeezes in and Cole puts his arm around him.

COLE
Hey, buddy.

INT. PARENTS' HOUSE / DINING ROOM - NIGHT

Each seat at the table is taken except one. Amanda's Dad can be seen standing in the family room, monitoring the TV. Plates are mostly empty as people scrape chocolate from them.

COLE
(to Amanda)
I don't know how you handle this. I can
walk onstage in front of thousands of
fans and not get nervous. Easy!
But today? My belly has been Butterfly
City.

AMANDA
You've seen the cuts. You did great!

COLE
Well, true, but—

Everyone laughs.

COLE
No, I did okay. But I know people will
judge me differently because I'm a
musician.

NATALIE
(to Amanda)
Why would anyone do that?

Amanda throws a napkin at her.

AMANDA'S DAD
It's on! Come on, come on!

INT. PARENTS' HOUSE / FAMILY ROOM - NIGHT

Amanda and Cole sit on a love-seat facing the TV. Patrick sits on the floor at his mom's feet. Everyone else sits on either a couch, dining room chairs, or the floor. Most of them hold coffee cups and Amanda's Dad enters with a coffee pot.

AMANDA'S DAD
Refills, anyone?

COLE
Please.

Cole holds out his mug. Amanda's Dad tops it off.

COLE
Thank you.

Onscreen, in the bed-and-breakfast living room, Amanda unwraps the old radio.

JESSICA
This is it! It's coming up!

NATALIE
Kissy, kissy!

Patrick smiles and runs from the room.

PATRICK
Time to go to the bathroom!

Amanda rests her forehead on Cole's shoulder. He sees that her eyes are shut.

Cole sets down his mug.

COLE
If you'll excuse us, Ms. Fox has a
tradition of not watching these scenes.

AMANDA'S MOM
Oh, just this once!

Cole stands up and offers his hand. Amanda takes it and stands.

COLE
Traditions are important to both of us.

AMANDA
Thank you.
But first, I need you to stand…right…
here.

As if posing him for a photo, Amanda squares his shoulders, then holds his hands, looks into his eyes, and starts laughing. Hysterically laughing.

Everyone—especially Cole—looks confused, then amused.

COLE
What is so—?

From outside the window a camera flashes.

COLE
Are you kidding me?!
(to Amanda)
I did not tell anyone I was coming here.
I swear on—!

COLE'S MOM
You better not say what I think you're
going to say.

*Patrick enters through the front door. Off Cole's expression, he holds
up a cameraphone.*

PATRICK
Mom told me to!

COLE
(to Amanda)
Care to explain?

AMANDA
(sheepishly)
I made a deal.
If Miss Heartbreaker left us alone for the
holidays, she could be the one to break
the story.

Cole smiles.

COLE
And the story is...?

AMANDA
Us.

Patrick hands Amanda the phone.

*ON CAMERAPHONE: A through-the-window shot of Amanda
laughing and Cole smiling at her.*

COLE
So, we're a story now?

Smiling, Amanda types on her phone.

AMANDA
We will be.

COLE
Why didn't you tell me he was taking
our picture?

AMANDA
To look natural, even the best actors
need help sometimes.

On TV, Amanda leaves the radio to answer the door.

JESSICA
You're heading to the porch!

Amanda puts the phone in her pocket and takes Cole's hand.

AMANDA
Shall we?

EXT. PARENTS' HOUSE / FRONT YARD - NIGHT

Amanda and Cole, holding hands, walk away from the closed front door. It's not currently snowing, but the ground is covered with it. Through the front window, their family and friends continue to watch the couple on TV talk on the porch of the bed-and-breakfast.

Outside, Amanda's phone beeps.

She pulls her phone from her back pocket and reads a text as they walk.

AMANDA
She says thank you and she wishes us a
very merry Christmas.

She puts the phone back in her pocket.

COLE
We're finally walking together in real
snow.

AMANDA
I think a lot of things feel more real.

*They walk a few more steps in silence and then stop to face each
other.*

AMANDA
Unlike that couple on TV, it isn't
snowing at the moment, real or fake.

Cole looks up. The stars are beautiful.

COLE
Also, no mistletoe.

*On TV (seen through the window), Amanda looks up at the
mistletoe.*

*Outside, Cole and Amanda look at each other as their TV versions
kiss.*

AMANDA
So, Mr. Actor, do you need a script to
tell you what to do next?

Through the window, Patrick looks out at them, kneeling where

Amanda and Cole were sitting. On TV, a slowly appearing script writes across the kissing couple: "THE END."

COLE
Care if I improvise a bit?

AMANDA
Please.

Cole and Amanda kiss.

Their family and friends join Patrick at the window.

Scripted letters slowly write across the kissing couple:

"The End"

Fade out.

"UNDER THE MISTLETOE"
BY JOANMARIE

[to play over credits]

Oh, the mistletoe
Is hanging low
As the wind blows the treetops
Dusted all with snow
So come on, my dear
Stand a little nearer
Let's let our toes touch
Under the mistletoe

[CHORUS]
Under the mistletoe
Don't you know in the snow
There ain't rules like we had in school
Your hand in mine intertwine
Yeah, I'm feeling fine
Anything goes under the mistletoe

We've been too busy
Just tryin' to make a living
Getting all the gifts wrapped
Hanging the Christmas star
So let's take a minute
Let ourselves be in it
If you want some romance
You don't have to look too far

[CHORUS]

LISTEN

The first official cover-version
of "Under the Mistletoe"
is performed by Trey Pearson
and can be found on YouTube.

It is awesome.

Made in the
USA
Middletown, DE